Franklin's Blanket

For two special children, Annie and Madeline — P. B.

For Linda, Derek and Stephanie, who had their own
special blankets — B. C.

Franklin is a trademark of Kids Can Press Ltd.

Kids Can Press acknowledges the financial support of the Ontario Arts
Council, the Canada Council for the Arts and the Government of
Canada, through the BPIDP, for our publishing activity.

Published in Canada by
Kids Can Press Ltd.
29 Birch Avenue
Toronto, ON M4V 1E2

Published in the U.S. by
Kids Can Press Ltd.
2250 Military Road
Tonawanda, NY 14150

www.kidscanpress.com

Printed and bound in China

The hardcover edition of this book is smyth sewn casebound.
The paperback edition of this book is limp sewn with a drawn-on cover.

CM 95 0 9 8 7 6 5
CDN PA 95 20 19 18 17 16 15 14 13 12 11 10

Canadian Cataloguing in Publication Data

Bourgeois, Paulette
    Franklin's blanket

ISBN 978-1-55074-154-4 (bound) ISBN 978-1-55074-278-7 (pbk.)

I. Clark, Brenda. II. Title.

PS8553.0874F75 1995   jC813'.54   C95-930636-6
PZ7.B787Fran 1995

Kids Can Press is a **Lorus** Entertainment company

Franklin's Blanket

Written by Paulette Bourgeois
Illustrated by Brenda Clark

Kids Can Press

FRANKLIN could slide down a riverbank all by himself. He could count by twos and tie his shoes. He could even sleep alone — as long as he had a goodnight story, a goodnight hug, a glass of water, a night light and his blue blanket.

In the beginning, the blanket was big and soft and edged in satin. But with all the snuggling and cuddling, it now had holes in the middle and tatters along the edges. Every year, as Franklin got bigger, his blue blanket got smaller.

Franklin usually kept his blanket folded in his top drawer. One night it wasn't there. Franklin searched around his room. He rummaged through his toy chest. He took everything out of his drawers and his books off the shelves. But he could not find his blue blanket anywhere.

He ran to tell his parents.

"Go back to bed," they said as soon as they saw him.

"But, but … " said Franklin.

"No buts," said Franklin's father. "You have had a goodnight story, a goodnight hug, two glasses of water, and I turned on your night light myself."

"But I can't find my blanket," said Franklin.

So Franklin and his parents hunted everywhere.
"Try to remember," said Franklin's mother. "When did you last have it?"

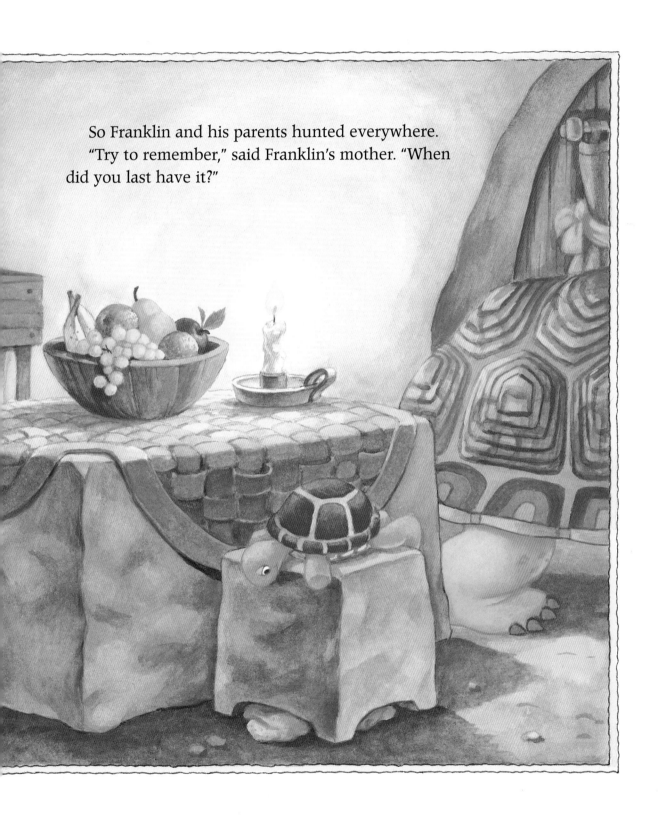

Franklin thought.

In the morning, after a fight with Bear, Franklin had snuggled with the blanket until he felt better.

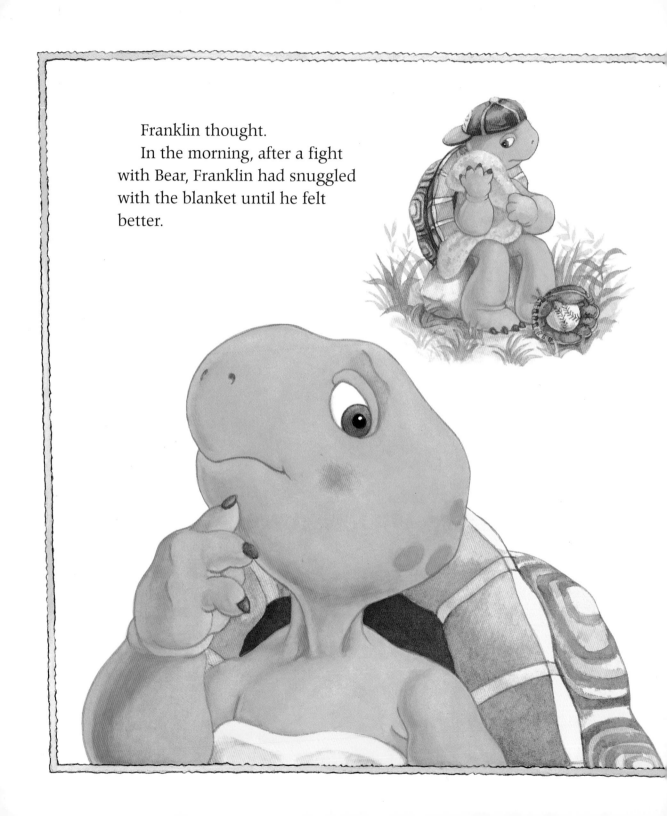

In the afternoon, when thunder crashed and lightning flashed, Franklin had covered himself with the blanket until all was calm.

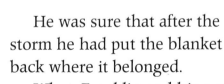

He was sure that after the storm he had put the blanket back where it belonged.

When Franklin and his parents looked, the blanket wasn't there.

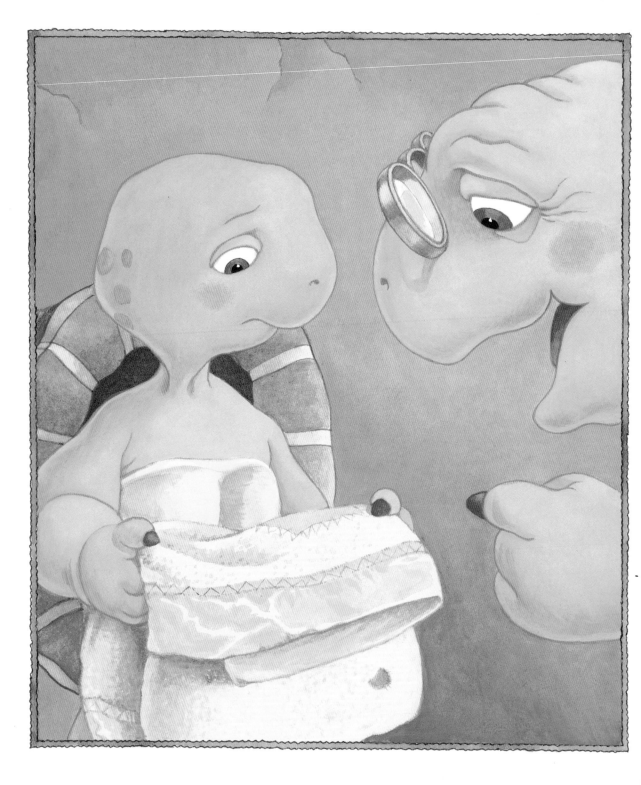

"We'll find it tomorrow," said Franklin's mother.

"I can't sleep without my blanket," said Franklin.

"I have an idea," said Franklin's father. He left the room and came back with an old, yellow blanket.

"What's that?" asked Franklin.

"It was mine," said Franklin's father. "Maybe it will make you feel better."

Franklin tried to snuggle the old, yellow blanket, but it wasn't the same. He missed his own blanket terribly, and it took Franklin a long, long time to fall asleep.

The next morning Franklin began a search for his blanket. He went to Bear's house first. He looked so glum that Bear asked, "What's wrong, Franklin? Did your mother give you brussels sprouts again?"

"Worse," said Franklin. "I can't find my blanket."

"It's not here," said Bear. "Besides, my mother says big bears like me are too old for baby blankets. Maybe you don't need a blanket."

Franklin knew that Bear always slept with his stuffed bunny. "What about your bunny?" asked Franklin.

"Bunnies are different," said Bear.

Next he tried Fox's house. The blanket wasn't there either.

"Why don't we play?" asked Fox.

"No," said Franklin. "I want to find my blanket."

"My father says worn-out blankets are no good to anybody," said Fox. "Maybe you should get a new blanket. I did."

"I like my old blanket," said Franklin.

Then Franklin went to Beaver's house. The blanket wasn't there. Franklin looked so sad that Beaver said, "You can borrow my Teddy until you find your blanket."

"Thank you, Beaver," said Franklin, holding Teddy tightly.

That night when Franklin went to bed, he had his father's yellow blanket and Beaver's Teddy. But it wasn't the same as sleeping with his own blue blanket.

At breakfast, Franklin's father sniffed and pinched his nose. "Do you smell something odd?" he asked. "A sort of musty, old-sock smell?"

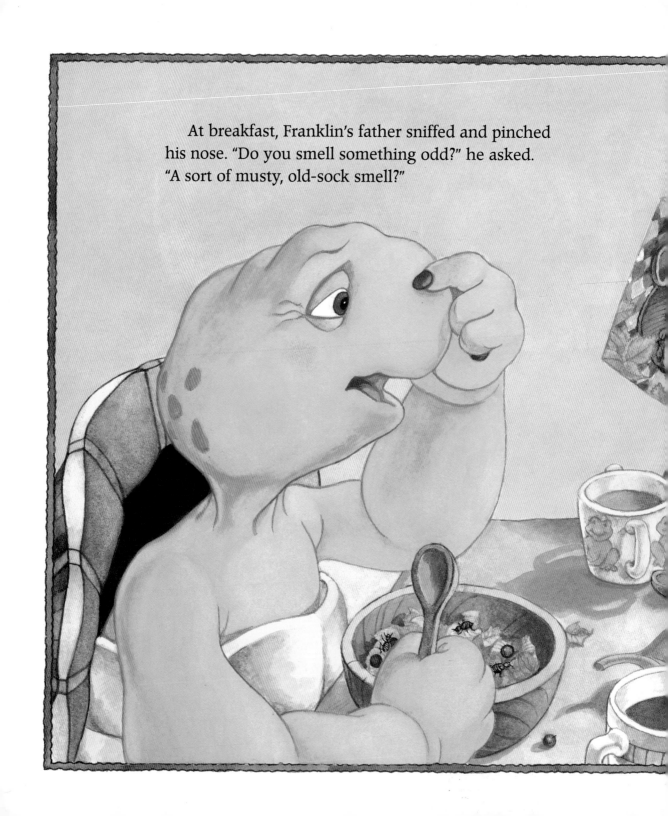

Franklin and his mother sniffed, too.
Then Franklin remembered. "I think I know
what smells," he said.

Franklin reached under his chair and pulled out his blue blanket. Plop! A handful of cold, slimy brussels sprouts spilled out of the blanket and onto the floor.

His mother and father stared with amazement.

"Look!" said Franklin. "I found my blanket. I forgot I put it here."

"You forgot to eat your brussels sprouts, too," said Franklin's mother.

"Whoops," said Franklin, looking a little sheepish.

"Old, cold brussels sprouts sure do stink," said Franklin's father.

"All brussels sprouts stink," said Franklin.

Franklin's mother smiled. "I used to hate cabbage," she said. "Now *that's* a stinky vegetable."

"Asparagus!" said Franklin's father. "That's even stinkier than brussels sprouts and cabbage mixed together."

"Broccoli!" shouted Franklin. Then he stopped. He liked broccoli. "It stinks, but I wouldn't hide broccoli," he said.

"That's good news," said his father.

Franklin helped to tidy the mess.

Then Franklin picked up his blanket.
"I don't care that you are old and full of holes,"
he said. "But you sure do need a bath."

That night, before his goodnight story, his
goodnight hug and a glass of water, Franklin put
his father's yellow blanket back where it belonged.
He was glad he lived in a house where even old
blankets had their special place.